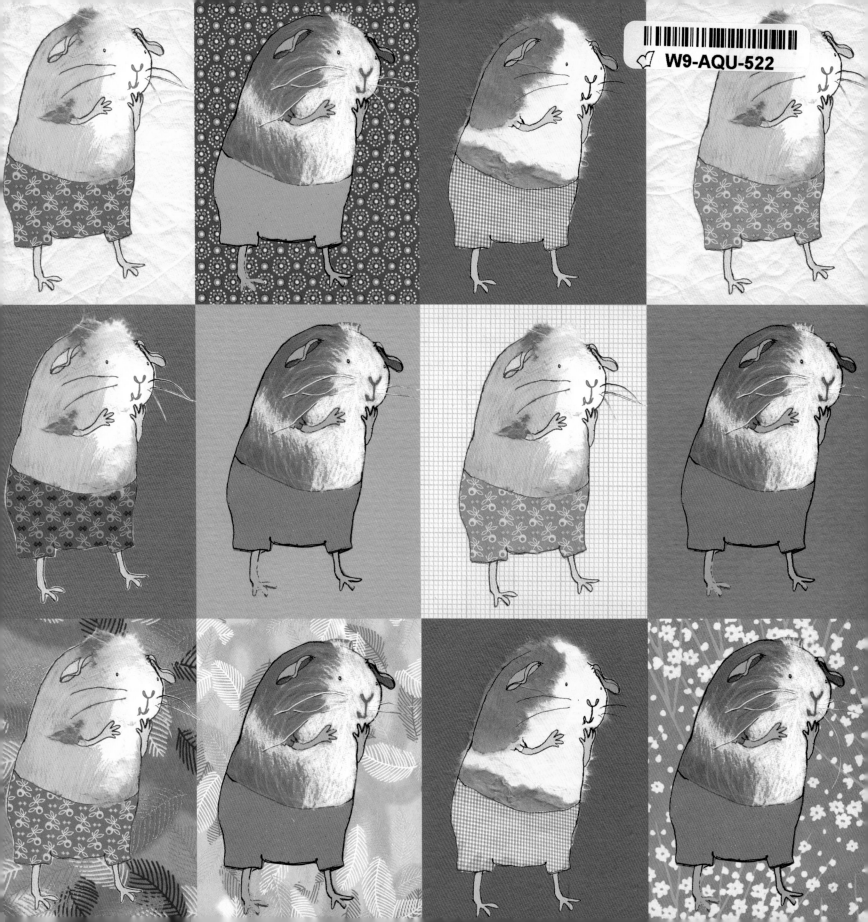

For Betty and Jack, with fond memories

Nicola and Charlotte

Text and illustrations copyright © 2009 by Charlotte Middleton
Nibbles: A Green Tale was originally published in the UK in 2009 as **Christopher Nibble**.
This edition is published by arrangement with Oxford University Press.
First Marshall Cavendish edition, 2010

Marshall Cavendish Corporation
99 White Plains Road
Tarrytown, NY 10591
www.marshallcavendish.us/kids

Library of Congress Cataloging-in-Publication Data
Middleton, Charlotte.
Nibbles : a green tale / Charlotte Middleton. – 1st ed.
p. cm.
Summary: Every guinea pig in Dandeville loves to eat dandelion leaves until there is only one plant left,
and Nibbles secretly and carefully tends this treasure until he can share the seeds with his community.
ISBN 978-0-7614-5791-6
[1. Plant conservation–Fiction. 2. Dandelions–Fiction. 3. Guinea pigs–Fiction.] I. Title.
PZ7.M5845Nib 2010
[E]–dc22
2009028902

The illustrations are rendered in mixed media.
Book design by Virginia Pope
Editor: Robin Benjamin

Paper used in the production of this book is a natural,
recyclable product made from wood grown in sustainable forests.
The manufacturing process conforms to the environmental regulations of the country of origin.

Printed in China (P)
10 9 8 7 6 5 4 3 2 1

mc **Marshall Cavendish**
Children

Nibbles

A Green Tale

by Charlotte Middleton

Marshall Cavendish Children

If there was one thing Nibbles **loved** more than soccer,

it was . . .

eating dandelion leaves.

He ate
dandelion leaves ...

at breakfast
time,

at lunch
time,

and at
dinner time.

And if Nibbles
felt hungry between meals,
he ate ...

more dandelion leaves!
But it was not just Nibbles who liked
dandelion leaves. Mr. and Mrs. Nibbles liked them.
His sister liked them. His friends liked them.

In fact ... every guinea pig
in Dandeville **loved** dandelion leaves.

munch

munch

nibble

munch

nibble

All day long the happy
sound of munching and
nibbling filled the air ...

until, that is, dandelion leaves began to run out.

Dandelion dishes were taken off the menus, and dandelion drinks disappeared from the shelves.

Menu Today

Carrot and lettuce wrap on a bed of ~~dandelion~~ leaves cabbage

~~Dandelion~~ soup cabbage ~~cabbage~~

~~Dandelion~~ and broccoli quiche

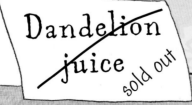

Dandelion ~~juice~~ sold out

Soon the worst thing imaginable happened....

All over town the dandelions had been munched to nothing more than bitten-down stalks, and the guinea pigs had to make do...

with chewy cabbage instead!

Just one dandelion was left but nobody knew about it, except Nibbles. It happened to be growing right outside his bedroom window.

Nibbles' mouth
watered at the sight of it.
But he knew he must not eat it,
or let anyone else eat it,
not if it was the last dandelion in town.

It might even be the last dandelion
in the whole world!
He thought hard and decided . . .

Cooking

THE VERY HUNGRY GRUB
JAMIE CAULIFLOWER
CHEESE PLEASE
Pippi Parsnip
Ready, Steady, Nibble
101 Lettuce Recipes
Hollyhock Magic!
GORDON RHUBARB
PRIDE & POISON
NIBBLES' CHRISTMAS
DAN DE LEON
The Oriental Cabbage
MONTY POIS
WAR & PIZZA

...to go to the library.

Sports

The Tour de Dandeville
MINI GOLF
MARATHON MOUSE
FOOTBALL MAD
SOCCER
CYCLING FOR GERBILS

Flowers   **Weeds**

Dandelions

Gardening
Shoots, Leaves & Weeds
LAWN EATING EXPERT
Brassica Breeding

WEEDS
the A–Z of

THE VERY HUNGRY GUINEA PIG

Bugs

THE WAY OF THE BUG

THE BIG GRUB Book

SUPER SNAILS

The Wonderful World of Worms

QUIET PLEASE!

He borrowed a book called
Everything You Need to Know about Dandelions

and he read it very carefully.

He found a little cover to protect his dandelion . . .

and every day he watered it and picked off the bugs.

Every day he was very good about not taking even the tiniest little nibble while he . . .

waited,
and waited,
and waited.

Until, finally, his dandelion had grown the most beautiful white head of tiny seeds.

Very **gently,**
Nibbles picked it
and carried it
all the way up
Daisy Chain Hill.
When he reached
the top . . .

he had just
enough puff to take
a deep breath and . . .

The seeds filled the air...

and landed gently all over Dandeville.

At first nobody noticed.

But soon the new
plants started to sprout
fresh leaves.

And in no time at all Dandeville
was filled with the happy sound
of munching once more.

As for Nibbles,

he still **loves** playing soccer.

munch

nibble

nibble

But now there's something he loves just as much as **eating** dandelions . . .

Nibbles loves **growing** them!

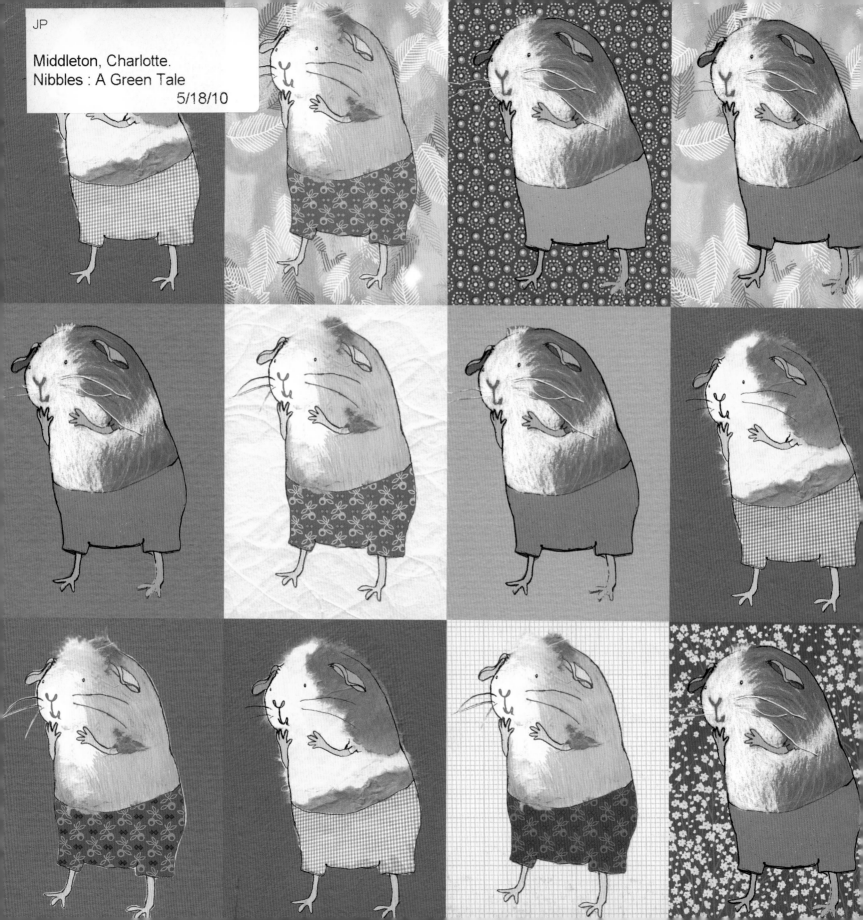